THE ELEPHANTS' EARS

written by Catherine Chambers
illustrated by Caroline Mockford

Barefoot Books
Celebrating Art and Story

At the foot of a snow-covered mountain,
there lived a mother elephant.
She had two young calves,
a boy called Palo and
a girl called Mala.

And they looked almost the
same, except that Palo had
small, neat ears and Mala
had wide, flapping ears.

Palo and Mala played happily all day long. Palo shared mangoes with the baboons in the forests at the foot of the mountain. Mala ran with the zebra that raced across the hot, dry grasslands.

In the evening, as the shadows grew longer, Palo and Mala made their way home. Mother elephant found them a safe place to rest for the night.

There, Mala tossed and turned, while Palo snuggled down and fell fast asleep.

The young elephants grew fast.
They stopped playing with the animals
that roamed around the mountain.
It was soon time for them to go out
into the world and live their own lives.

Mother elephant watched
them closely, shaking her
head sadly and whisking
her tail.
"Oh, Palo and Mala! You are so very different
from each other," she said.
"I just don't know what kind of life will be
best for you both."

"Aaaaaaa," crooned mother elephant, nodding her head at Palo. "You with your neat little ears and soft, gentle ways. You will be happiest in a place where you can work hard and live peacefully."

"Aaaaoooo!"
she trumpeted,
shaking her head at Mala.
"You with your grand,
flapping ears, and
wild, wild ways.
You will be happiest in a place
where you can feel free."

Mother elephant rocked from side to side, thinking hard. She watched Palo collecting piles of leaves and bark for the family's lunch, while Mala rolled happily in a muddy pool.

Then, mother elephant looked
up and saw a tiny black dot circling
the mountain top. It was the
giant black eagle, kind and wise.
Now mother elephant knew
exactly what to do.
She lifted her trunk and roared,
"Oh, Queen of the Mountain, please help
me to find a place for Palo and Mala
in the great, wide world."

The tiny black dot stopped suddenly,
and swooped and whirled down
the mountain toward mother
elephant. The great eagle settled
on a thorn tree, her black satin wings
shining in the hot sun.
"I heard your cry,"
said the great eagle.
"And I will search the world to find
a home for Palo and Mala
Trust me."

She flapped her wide wings, blowing the dust into a billowing red cloud. Then she began to circle the earth.

The great eagle looked down and saw vast oceans and huge mountain ranges. But more than this, she saw a piece of the earth cut in the shape of Palo's ear. Moving westward, she spied a piece of the earth cut in the shape of Mala's ear.

With great excitement, the wise eagle made her
way back to the mountain.
As she flew, she called upon a white egret and a
pink flamingo to follow her.
Sitting once more in the thorn tree,
the Queen of the Mountain called Palo and Mala
to her side.

"Now," she said. "I have searched the whole
earth. But I haven't found a place where Palo and
Mala can live together." Mother elephant shook
her head sadly. "But," continued the wise eagle,
"I have found two homes where each of them
can find happiness."

The great eagle turned to Palo. "Now, Palo,"
she said. "I have found the perfect place
for you. Follow the white egret.
He will lead you there."

She turned to Mala. "Now, Mala," she said. "I have found the perfect place for you. Just follow the pink flamingo. He will lead you there."

Mother elephant knew that it was time for Palo and Mala to leave their home. She wrapped her long trunk around them and held them both tight.

"Goodbye, Palo," she said. "Be fair and wise.

Goodbye, Mala. Be kind and strong." And with a long, loud trumpet, mother elephant finally let them go.

Palo walked and walked
until the white egret
spied land in the shape
of Palo's ear.

It was India. There
Palo stopped.

Mala walked and walked until the pink flamingo spied land in the shape of Mala's ear. It was Africa. There Mala stopped.

In his new home, Palo learned how
to clear the narrow paths that
wound around the tall trees.
He learned how to walk carefully
with children on his back.

Other elephants just like Palo
found their way to the forests of India.
Palo taught them all he knew.
And he became a wise judge among them.

In her new home, Mala learned how to find plenty of food and cool pools of water. At night, she found the safest places to rest. She learned how to protect her calves from the dangers of the plains.

Other elephants just like Mala found
their way to the grasslands of Africa.

Mala taught them all she knew.
And she became a great leader among them.

And that is how the Indian elephant,
with its neat ears and quiet ways,
and the African elephant,
with its grand ears
and excitable ways,
found their
homelands.

AFRICAN AND INDIAN ELEPHANTS

Today, African elephants roam in small herds across the grasslands of east, central and southern Africa. The Indian, or Asian, elephant lives in the forests of India and South East Asia. In the grasslands and forests, both types of elephant gather leaves, bark and branches to eat.

Elephants have a close family life. The herds are made up mostly of females and calves. Male elephants are called bulls. Female elephants in the herd help to look after a mother elephant's calf. African mother elephants flap their huge ears onto their backs to call their children.

An elephant's trunk can pull out small trees. It can carry loads. Or it can be used as a hose. The trunk sucks up water and squirts it into the animal's mouth. Or it washes down the elephant's back to keep it cool. Inside the trunk, the African elephant has two fingers which can pick up quite small objects. The Indian elephant has one finger. Elephants have a very good sense of smell, too.

Near the African elephant's trunk grow two long tusks, made of smooth, cream-colored ivory. For hundreds of years, craftsmen have carved this ivory into fine jewelry and ornaments. But to get the ivory tusks, hunters have killed hundreds of thousands of elephants, so the hunting of elephants in Africa has been banned.

The African elephant cannot be tamed, but the Indian elephant can be trained to use its trunk to pick up logs and other goods. It has also been taught how to carry loads on its back. In this way, the Indian elephant works for human beings.

Catherine Chambers

Barefoot Books 2067 Massachusetts Avenue, Cambridge, MA 02140
Text copyright © 2000 Catherine Chambers. Illustrations copyright © 2000 by Caroline Mockford.
The moral right of Catherine Chambers to be identified as the author and Caroline Mockford to be identified as the illustrator of this work has been asserted. First published in the United States of America in 2000 by Barefoot Books, Inc. All right reserved. No part of this book may be reproduced in any form or by any means, electronic or mechanical, including photocopying, recording, or by any information storage and retrieval system, without permission in writing from the publisher. This book is printed on 100% acid-free paper. This book was typeset in Kabel Demi 20 on 26 point leading. The illustrations were prepared in acrylics on 140lb watercolor paper.
Graphic design by Judy Linard, England. Color separation by Grafiscan, Italy.
Printed and bound in Hong Kong by South China Printing Co. Ltd.
3 5 7 9 8 6 4
U.S. Cataloging-in-Publication Data   (Library of Congress Standards)
Chambers, Caroline.
    The elephants' ears/ written by Catherine Chambers, illustrated by
Caroline Mockford. —1st ed.
[32] p. : col. Ill. ; cm.
Summary: Palo and Mala, two little elephants, need to live in places which will suit their distinct characters, and so their mother begins a search for the lands where they will be happiest. The story shows that being different is not bad, each can be loved for their uniqueness. Includes information about Indian and African elephants.
ISBN: 1-84148-249-8
1. Parental acceptance – Fiction. 2 Social acceptance --- Fiction. I Mockford, Caroline, ill. II Title.
[E] –dc21   1999   AC   CIP